EXOTIC

IGNORANCE

Looking 4 An African Prince

I need a man that doesn't have a sense of self and can treat me right.

Serious Inquiries Only.

African Prince In Search Of A
Peaceful Sistah

My last girlfriend was neurotic and
clingy. She controlled everything
in the household and would fly
into a rage whenever I offered a
different perspective. Are you
psychologically sound?

Peaceful Sistah Looking For A Psychologist/Platonic Friend

I use to be so peaceful. Now I notice that I have anxiety issues. I'm suspicious of everyone even my family. I was hurt so badly.

Please help.

Psychologist Looking For Drug
Dealer

I can't listen to people's problems
anymore. It's draining. After my
last session, I got high in the
bathroom. Not the first time. I
prayed as I got high. I asked for
God's forgiveness. I need some
stronger meds.

I don't want to lose my license. I'm looking for a discreet encounter. Game on!

Drug Dealer Looking For A Place To Escape Preferably A Mansion

Someone's chasing me. A Psychologist tried to stiff me out of my chicken (money). Then, someone was lurking and started firing shots.

I ran and hid for several hours. I need a place to crash. My standards are high.

Maria Searching For Bodybuilder Boyfriend

Good Morning. I'm looking for a buff bodybuilder to be my boyfriend. He needs to help me get this criminal out of my home. The only thing he does is sleep. Drugs are always dropping from his pockets at night. He tells me "it's a new product from a B2B marketing company."

Bodybuilder Seeks Woman Of The Cloth

I've been geeking off these drugs. Me and my girlfriend need help. I was raised in a religious household. I'm having depressive thoughts and psychotic episodes. I prefer a woman since I don't take kindly to male authority.

Pastor Seeking Someone to Help
Look For Bodybuilder

I welcomed him into my church
and home. He stole the pulpit and
gold crosses. A church staff
member told me that he sold
everything online including his
girlfriend. Help me find this man.

Athlete Finds Suspect

I found the guy for the Pastor. The thief and I scrapped for an hour. I have some bruises and my muscles are sore. Aye Pastor where's the $$$ for my good deed?

I need a gorgeous lady for a massage and to help calm me down. Also, I have a basketball game tomorrow and I don't want to oversleep. I'll pay you $50 for the massage, $25 for a happy ending and $25 for waking me up with morning kisses. Contact me ASAP.

Social Worker Seeks Immediate Help

Hi. I can't believe I ended up sleeping with someone on here. I hope you're not to worn out for ya game. JERK!!! He gave me fake money and an STD. I need someone to call my husband and tell him that I can't make the banquet tonight I have to fly to Peru to help ghostwrite a book for a client.

Must be believable.

Women only.

Anonymous Women Needs Help With Book

I need someone to help me write a book about a woman that cheated on her husband with someone online. I can't use my name because she made me sign a confidentiality agreement.

Payment is negotiable. You will receive a bonus if this is made into a movie.

Must be willing to be my secret lover so I can reenact what took place in the story.

Men only.

Secret Lover Looking For Room

Neighbors called the police after hearing screams and yells during passionate sex. I'm Black. She's white. The Police are downstairs. They'll interrogate her, but kill me. I need a temporary place to stay if I make it out of this.

Gender not important.

RE: Secret Lover Looking For Room

You and the Nigger Bitch deserve to die!

RE RE: Secret Lover Looking For Room

Dude's busy being surrounded by 12. I got time to physically address your White Supremacy. Up your email cave beast, so we can't shoot the fair one offline.

RE RE RE: Secret Lover Looking
For Room

BLACK POWER!!!!

RE RE RE RE: Secret Lover Looking For Room

In the bedroom, he should have used a high-pitched voice when deploying his troops inside the dark alley.

RE RE RE RE RE: Secret Lover
Looking For Room

All of a sudden, everybody's pro
black and a sex expert on the
internet nowadays. SMH. Btw,
ALL LIVES MATTER.

RE RE RE RE RE RE: Secret Lover Looking For Room

Nigga, I'm pro black wherever I am. You're a Niggacoon.

RE RE RE RE RE RE RE: Secret Lover Looking For Room

Nigga said all lives matter. We're the ones getting murdered every day.

RE RE RE RE RE RE RE RE:
Secret Lover Looking For Room

We need to start banning coons
from this site.

RE RE RE RE RE RE RE RE RE: Secret Lover Looking For Room

How do we know he's a Nigga or a coon. You can be anyone on here.

RE RE RE RE RE RE RE RE
RE RE: Secret Lover Looking For
A Room

Why are we still using the N
word? Can't we use King or
Brotha to describe us.

RE RE RE RE RE RE RE RE
RE RE RE: Secret Lover Looking
For Room

What about us women? All
women's lives matter.

RE RE RE RE RE RE RE RE
RE RE RE RE: Secret Lover
Looking For Room

If the black man is exterminated,
then black women will be the
servants or casualties of white
supremacy.

RE RE RE RE RE RE RE RE
RE RE RE RE RE: Secret Lover
Looking For Room

KINGBROTHANIGGA
YOU'RE BLACK!

RE RE RE RE RE RE RE RE
RE RE RE RE RE RE :Secret
Lover Looking For Room

Why you gotta take it there? You
make us black people look bad.

RE RE RE RE RE RE RE RE RE RE RE RE RE RE RE: Secret Lover Looking For Room

If you want revolutionary and black empowerment talk then go to another site. I'm contacting the moderator.

This section is for finding a soulmate and hot in the pants females. Peace.

RE RE RE RE RE RE RE RE
RE RE RE RE RE RE RE RE:
Secret Lover Looking For Room

Get your thirsty ass coonass out
of here. And back to that other
clown.

Your momma raised you huh? Because you sound real sensitive and soft.

RE RE RE RE RE RE RE RE RE RE RE RE RE RE RE RE RE: Secret Lover Looking For Room

My momma raised me and I turned into a strong black man. My father never did anything for me and when we're in the same vicinity we barely speak. I think he's jealous because I became the man he wanted to be.

RE RE RE RE RE RE RE RE
RE RE RE RE RE RE RE RE
RE RE: Secret Lover Looking For
Room

Hey everyone, this is the moderator. I need everyone to focus on relationship content only.

RE RE RE RE RE RE RE RE
RE RE RE RE RE RE RE RE
RE RE RE: Secret Lover Looking
For Room

Keep it a band pet nigga, the
White Man runs this site that's
why you're scared. He pays your
salary.

You live up the block from me.
You probably been a house nigga
since kindergarten.

RE RE RE RE RE RE RE RE
RE RE RE RE RE RE RE RE
RE RE RE RE: Secret Lover
Looking For Room

Why are we arguing and debating on here? Let's build and help our Brotha get out of this predicament.

RE RE RE RE RE RE RE RE
RE RE RE RE RE RE RE RE
RE RE RE RE RE: Secret Lover
Looking For Room

Oh shit, they sent the whole police
force to get this brotha. Shits like
a movie. Ya'll watching?

RE RE RE RE RE RE RE RE
RE RE RE RE RE RE RE RE
RE RE RE RE RE RE: Secret
Lover Looking For Room

Ya'll coons can't build anything. Ya'll don't have the intelligence. We Fathered ya'll backwards people. You can't do nothing without our permission. All Hail The Whiteman.

RE RE RE RE RE RE RE RE
RE RE RE RE RE RE RE RE
RE RE   RE RE RE RE RE:
Secret Lover Looking For Room

White people couldn't make the
economy prosperous without
stealing our talents and resources.

RE RE RE RE RE RE RE RE
RE RE RE RE RE RE RE RE
RE RE RE RE RE RE RE RE:
Secret Lover Looking For Room

Let's stop talking and start doing.
All the action takers connect with
me via email. Put Exotic
Ignorance in the subject line so I
know it isn't spam.

RE RE RE RE RE RE RE RE
RE RE RE RE RE RE RE RE
RE RE RE RE RE RE RE RE
RE: Secret Lover Looking For
Room

Oh shit, they just murked son on
air.

RE RE RE RE RE RE RE RE
RE RE RE RE RE RE RE RE
RE RE RE RE RE RE RE RE
RE RE RE: Secret Lover Looking
For Room

I keep telling brothas, these white
girls gonna get them assassinated.

RE RE RE RE RE RE RE RE
RE RE RE RE RE RE RE RE
RE RE RE RE RE RE RE RE
RE RE RE RE: Secret Lover
Looking For A Room

That's why I'm getting my money
up so I can buy a sex bot with
blonde hair and blue eyes.

RE RE RE RE RE RE RE RE
RE RE RE RE RE RE RE RE
RE RE RE RE RE RE RE RE
RE RE:
Secret Lover Looking For Room

Who are these black people
surrounding the Pigs?

RE RE RE RE RE RE RE RE
RE RE RE RE RE RE RE RE
RE RE RE RE RE RE RE RE
RE RE RE: Secret Lover Looking
For Room

Link?

RE RE RE RE RE RE RE RE
RE RE RE RE RE RE RE RE
RE RE RE RE RE RE RE RE
RE RE RE RE: Secret Lover
Looking For Room

Wanna talk with beautiful hot superstar thotties in your local area today? Go to www. Thot Hots dot com and enter access code 901.

RE RE RE RE RE RE RE RE
RE RE RE RE RE RE RE RE
RE RE RE RE RE RE RE RE
RE RE RE RE RE: Secret Lover
Looking For Room

Come   watch   Rapper   Hoodie
Velour and Model Brittany
Comesporing X- rated London
Treehouse tape
@ www.finestxxxonline.com
Must be 18 or over

RE RE RE RE RE RE RE RE
RE RE RE RE RE RE RE RE
RE RE RE RE RE RE RE RE
RE RE RE RE RE RE: Secret
Lover Looking For Room

Bro, the link's below. Guess we really are living in the last days.
www.channelsliveinmotion.com

RE RE RE RE RE RE RE RE
RE RE RE RE RE RE RE RE
RE RE RE RE RE RE RE RE
RE RE RE RE RE RE RE: Secret
Lover Looking For Room

This dude with the megaphone
said "we are the African Elite
Lions" and he signaled his
comrades to start shooting. These
dudes are trained marxmen. Look,
look, they're everywhere.

RE RE RE RE RE RE RE RE
RE RE RE RE RE RE RE RE
RE RE RE RE RE RE RE RE
RE RE RE RE RE RE RE RE:
Secret Lover Looking For Room

Cot Damn. Shit's litty.

FBI WARNING

THIS SITE HAS BEEN SHUTDOWN DUE TO SUBVERSIVE AND POLITICAL PROPAGANDA

Email: <ins>concreteposture@gmail.com</ins>